SUGAR HERO

FRANKLIN PARK LIBRARY
FRANKLIN PARK, IL

STONE ARCH BOOKS
MINNEAPOLIS SAN DIEGO

Graphic Sparks are published by Stone Arch Books,
A Capstone Imprint
151 Good Counsel Drive, P.O. Box 669
Mankato, Minnesota 56002
www.capstonepub.com

Copyright © 2010 by Stone Arch Books

Library of Congress Cataloging-in-Publication Data

Dahl, Michael.
  Sugar hero / by Michael Dahl ; illustrated by Jeff Crowther.
     p. cm. -- (Graphic sparks. Princess Candy)
  ISBN 978-1-4342-1587-1 (lib. bdg.)
  ISBN 978-1-4342-2801-7 (pbk.)
  1. Graphic novels. [1. Graphic novels. 2. Superheroes--Fiction. 3.
Schools--Fiction.] I. Crowther, Jeff, ill. II. Title.
  PZ7.7.D34Su 2010
  741.5'973--dc22

                              2009011407

Summary: On Halo Nightly's eleventh birthday, her Aunt Pandora gives
her a collection of jars filled with brightly colored candies. Soon she
learns that the candies give her the incredible powers of nature.
Halo uses the powers to combat Doozie Hiss, a rival student with
superpowered hair.

Creative Director: Heather Kindseth
Designer: Brann Garvey

J-GN
PRINCESS CANDY
412-6572

Printed in the United States of America in Stevens Point, Wisconsin.
062011
006248R

PRINCESS CANDY

SUGAR HERO

WRITTEN BY
MICHAEL DAHL

ILLUSTRATED BY
JEFF CROWTHER

DOOZIE HISS

MR. SLINK

Midnight is a place.

A big, dark city.

And in one corner of Midnight City, in Midnight Elementary School . . .

Something weird is going on.

Something so scary . . .

MR. SLINK

Something so hairy . . .

That we can't even look!

Meanwhile, in another part of the busy metropolis . . .

Happy birthday, Halo!

Grandma! This cake is so cool!

I was hoping you'd like it.

It was on sale for half price at the Day Old Bakery Shop.

Be polite and ask Mr. Nussbaum if he'd like a piece.

8

Dear Halo,
You are my favorite niece. That is why I am giving you this special, secret gift. It was given to me long ago, on my eleventh birthday.

As you know, I am very sick. In case anything should happen to me, I have left this gift with Grandma. She will give it to you on YOUR eleventh birthday. Remember to use it wisely.

"Your loving aunt, Pandora."

Use it wisely? What does that mean?

14

15

Hi, Grandma. I'm almost finished with my homework. I'll be outside in a few minutes.

Good girl. I'll be parked by the front door.

I didn't find anything about Aunt Pandora's candy in the school's science books.

Maybe I'll go to the public library tomorr —

Hey, what's that!?

MR. SLINK

Thanks again for the ride, Grandma.

No problem, Halo.

Say, I have an idea.

How about us girls go to a salon tomorrow?

We could both get our hair done.

Hair?

About The Author

Michael Dahl is the author of more than 200 books for children and young adults. He has won the AEP Distinguished Achievement Award three times for his non-fiction. His Finnegan Zwake mystery series was shortlisted twice by the Anthony and Agatha awards. He has also written the Library of Doom series and the Dragonblood books. He is a featured speaker at conferences around the country on graphic novels and high-interest books for boys.

About The Illustrator

Jeff Crowther has been drawing comics for as long as he can remember. Since graduating from college, Jeff has worked on a variety of illustrations for clients including Disney, Adventures Magazine, and Boy's Life Magazine. He also wrote and illustrated the webcomic Sketchbook and has self-published several mini-comics. Jeff lives in Boardman, Ohio, with his wife, Elizabeth, and their children, Jonas and Noelle.

aqua (AH-kwah)—a Spanish word meaning "water"

average (AV-uh-rij)—usual, or ordinary

charcoal (CHAR-kole)—a form of carbon made from partially burned wood, often used as barbecue fuel

fuego (FWAY-go)—a Spanish word meaning "fire"

metropolis (meh-TRAH-poh-liss)—a large city

powerful (POU-ur-ful)—having great strength

pressure (PRESH-ur)—a burden or strain

property (PROP-ur-tee)—anything that is owned by an individual

salon (sah-LAHN)—a stylish business or shop

wisely (WIZE-lee)—to do something with good judgment

woozy (WOO-zee)—dizzy or mildly sick

Doozie

SUPER-VILLAIN

Villain Facts

First Appearance
Princess Candy: Sugar Hero

Real Name...............Medusa Marie Hiss

Occupation.....................Honor Student

Height............................4 feet 5 inches

Weight....................................75 pounds

Eyes..Black

Hair....................Green (and snake-like)

Special Powers
*Super-annoying personality; ability to
instantly transform into a teacher's pet;
living hair with deadly tentacle powers*

*Unable to have another child, Medusa's parents
spoiled their only daughter to the core. On
the morning of her third-grade class photo,
Medusa awoke to a particularly bad hair day.
Her mother, a genetic scientist, created a high-
tech hair gel to tame her child's unruly hairdo.
But after her father, an out-of-work hairdresser,
applied the prototype product, Medusa's hair
turned deadly. With her lizard locks, she had
become the evil and annoying . . . Doozie Hiss.*

Princess Puzzlers

Q: Where does the word "candy" come from?

A: The word "candy" comes from the Arabic word "qandi," which means "sugar."

Q: Who discovered chocolate?

A: People from the ancient cultures of Mexico and Central America made chocolate more than 2,000 years ago.

Q: Which state produces the most chocolate?

A: Pennsylvania makes more chocolate than any other state. It is home to the Hershey chocolate factory.

Discussion Question

1. Halo caught Doozie Hiss stealing the answers to a test. What do you think Doozie's punishment should be? Explain your answer.

2. Why do you think Aunt Pandora chose to give Halo the superpowered candy? What do you think she wanted Halo to do with them?

3. When she eats a piece of candy, Halo gains some amazing superpowers. If you could have just one superpower, what would it be? Explain.

WRITING PROMPTS

1. Think about your favorite candy. Now imagine that sweet treat could turn you into a superhero. Write about what you would do with your newfound powers.

2. At the end of the story, Halo leaves Doozie tied to the flagpole. Pretend you are the author and write a story about what happens next. Does Doozie escape? Is she punished for her crime?

3. Write your own Princess Candy comic. What kind of candy will Halo try next time? What super-villlain will she face? Use your imagination.

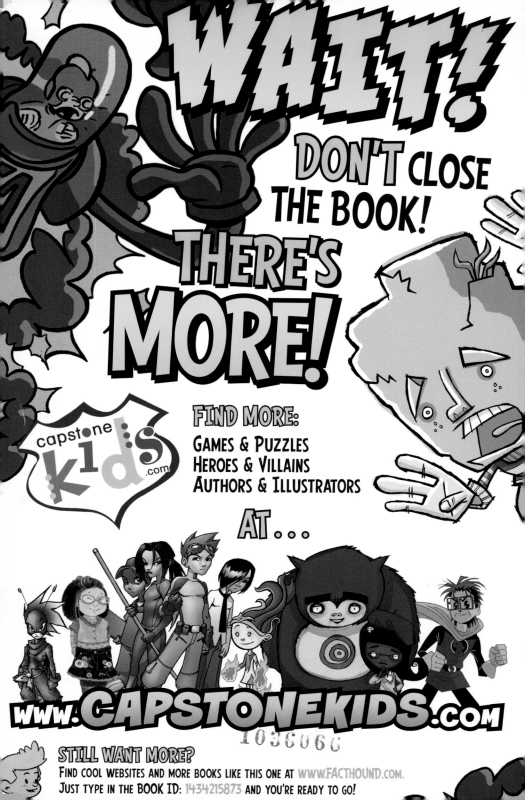